To The Rescue

A Red Fox Book

Published by Random House Children's Books
20 Vauxhall Bridge Road, London SW1V 2SA

A division of Random House UK Ltd
London Melbourne Sydney Auckland
Johannesburg and agencies throughout the world

1 3 5 7 9 10 8 6 4 2

This Junior Novel first published in Great Britain
by Red Fox 1999

Printed and bound in Norway by
AIT Trondheim AS

Papers used by Random House UK Limited are natural, recyclable products made from wood grownin sustainable forests. The manufacturing processes conform to the environmental regulations of the country of origin.

RANDOM HOUSE UK Limited Reg. No. 954009

ISBN 0 09 940442 7

DOCTOR DOLITTLE

TO THE RESCUE

From the stories by

HUGH LOFTING

Abridged by

CHARLIE SHEPPARD

RED FOX

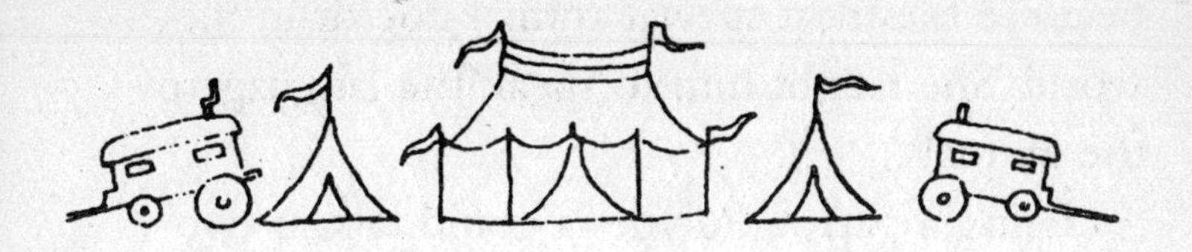

1. Introducing Doctor Dolittle

In the beginning Doctor Dolittle was an ordinary people's doctor. He prescribed pills and mended broken bones the way normal doctors do. But besides doctoring sick people, he also doctored animals.

Doctor Dolittle loved animals and animals loved him, and soon he had so many staying in his house there was barely room for a human patient to get in the front door. He had white mice in the piano, rabbits in the pantry, and a pig called Gub-Gub who slept in the vegetable bin. Even the airing cupboard was occupied by a family of squirrels.

When his human patients refused to come to him unless he got rid of the animals, Doctor Dolittle stopped doctoring humans entirely; he became an animal doctor only. And then one day Polynesia, the parrot who had become a member of the Doctor's household, helped him to become the most special animal doctor in the world. She taught him to speak the language of the animals.

Being a parrot, Polynesia could talk in two languages - people's language and animal language. She was able to explain to the Doctor the meanings of the nose-twitching, ear-scratching and tail-wagging signals that help the animals to talk to each other.

It wasn't long before Doctor Dolittle was able not only to understand what the animals were saying but to speak to them too. The animals were amazed to find a human who was keen to learn their languages, and very soon they understood him as well as they did their own animal friends.

Dab-Dab, the duck, became the Doctor's housekeeper. She cooked and scrubbed, dusted amd cleaned, and went to market twice a week to keep the larder filled with assorted foods for the Doctor's strange family.

The household accounts and the Doctor's business dealings were taken care of by Too-Too, the owl, who was a famous mathematician - among animals, of course.

Jip, the dog, was also very special to Doctor Dolittle. Whenever there was a job of scenting to be done, Jip had no equal. He could follow the trail of a man who was miles away, simply by identifying the tobacco the man smoked.

But perhaps the strangest creature who lived with the Doctor at Puddleby-on-the-Marsh was a two-headed animal called a pushmi-pullyu. He had a head at each end of his body and could eat with one while talking with the other. The pushmi-pullyu said this enabled him to avoid talking with his mouth full.

Of couse helping and feeding so many animals was an expensive business and soon Doctor Dolittle found himself penniless. One day he decided the only way he would ever be able to pay off his debts was if he joined the circus and put the incredible pushmi-pullyu on show. The pushmi-pullyu was delighted to be able to help his good friend and so this plan of action was agreed upon. This is the story of the adventures Doctor Dolittle had when he and his friends joined and travelled with the circus.

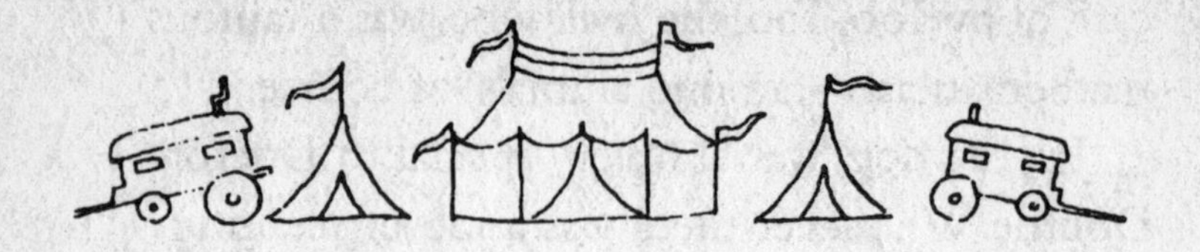

2. *Business Arrangements*

Doctor Dolittle decided he would ask Alexander Blossom, the famous ringmaster, to help him show the pushmi-pullyu. So Doctor Dolittle, and his dear friend, Matthew Mugg, set out for Blossom's Circus in Grimbledon. They found the ringmaster counting money at the gate.

John Dolittle described the wonderful pushmi-pullyu he had at home and said he wanted to join the circus with it. Alexander Blossom admited he would like to see this strange creature and he agreed to come to Puddleby-on-the-Marsh to look at it.

Matthew Mugg and Doctor Dolittle tramped back home, very pleased with their success so far. 'If you go with Blossom's Circus,' Matthew asked, 'will you take me and my wife with you, Doctor? I'd come in real handy, taking care of the caravan, feeding and cleaning and the likes o' that.'

'Of course, Matthew,' said the Doctor. 'You are both very welcome to come.'

Late that night, when the Grimbledon Fair had closed, Mr Blossom came to the Doctor's house in Puddleby-on-the-Marsh. After he had been shown by the light of a lantern the pushmi-pullyu grazing on the lawn, he came back into the library with the Doctor and said, 'How much do you want for that animal?'

'No, no, he's not for sale,' said the Doctor.

'Oh, come now,' said Blossom. 'You don't want him. Anyone could see you're not a regular showman. I'll give you twenty pounds for him.'

'No,' said the Doctor.

'Thirty pounds,' said Blossom.

Still the Doctor refused.

'Forty pounds - fifty pounds,' said Blossom. Then he went up and up, offering prices that made Matthew Mugg, who was listening, open his eyes wider and wider with wonder.

'It's no use,' said the Doctor at last. 'You must either take me with the animal into your circus or leave him where he is. I have promised that I myself will see he is properly treated.'

'What do you mean?' asked the showman. 'Ain't he your property? Who did you promise?'

'He's his own property,' said the Doctor. 'He came here to oblige me. It was to himself, the pushmi-pullyu, that I gave my promise.'

'What! Are you crazy?' asked the showman.

Matthew Mugg was going to explain to Blossom that the Doctor could speak animals' language, but John Dolittle motioned him to be silent.

'And so, you see,' he went on, 'you must either take me and the animal, or neither.'

Well, the upshot of it was that the showman finally consented to all the Doctor asked. The pushmi-pullyu and his party were to be provided with a new wagon all to themselves and, although travelling as part of the circus, were to be entirely free and independent. The money made was to be divided equally between the Doctor and Blossom. Whenever the pushmi-pullyu wanted a day off he was to have it, and whatever kind of food he asked for was to be provided by Blossom.

When all the arrangements had been gone into, Blossom said he would send a caravan the next day. 'Have your party ready by eleven in the morning. Good night.'

'Good night,' said the Doctor.

3. *The Doctor's New Home*

Very early the next morning Dab-Dab had the house closed and everybody waiting outside on the front steps hours before the wagon arrived.

At last Jip, who had been out scouting, came rushing back to the party gathered on the steps. 'The wagon's coming,' he panted, 'all red and yellow - it's just around the bend.'

Then everybody got excited and began grabbing their parcels. The wagon, when it finally came in sight, was certainly a thing of beauty. It was made like a gypsy caravan, with windows and a door and a chimney. It was very gaily painted and quite new.

They all piled in and reached the Grimbledon fairgrounds about two o'clock in the afternoon, entering the circus enclosure by a back gate. Inside the enclosure they found the great Blossom himself waiting to welcome them.

He seemed quite surprised, on the wagon's being opened, to find the odd collection of creatures the Doctor had brought with him - he was particularly astonished at the pig. However, he was so delighted to have the pushmi-pullyu that he didn't mind.

He at once led them to what he called their stand - which, he said, he had had built for them that very morning. Across the front of it was a sign:

THE PUSHMI-PULLYU!
COME AND SEE THE MARVELLOUS
TWO-HEADED ANIMAL
FROM THE JUNGLES OF AFRICA!
ADMISSION SIXPENCE

The red and yellow wagon (in which the Doctor's party, with the exception of the pushmi-pullyu, were to live) was backed behind the 'stand'. And Dab-Dab immediately set about making up beds and arranging the inside so it would be homelike.

After the pushmi-pullyu had been moved to his new home in the stand and the Doctor had seen that he was provided with hay and water and bedding, the Puddleby party started out to make a tour of the circus under the guidance of the great Alexander Blossom.

The main show took place only twice a day, in a big tent in the middle of the enclosure. But all around this there were smaller tents and stands, most of which you had to pay extra to get into. Of these, the pushmi-pullyu's stand was now to form one. The others contained all manner of wonders: shooting galleries, guessing games, bearded ladies, merry-go-rounds, strong men, snake charmers, a menagerie and many more.

The next day, the pushmi-pullyu was put on show for the first time. He was very popular. A two-headed animal had never before been seen in a circus and the people thronged up to pay their money and have a look at him. At first he nearly died of embarrassment and shyness, and he was forever hiding one of his heads under the straw so as not to have to meet the gaze of all those staring eyes. Then the people wouldn't believe he had more than one head, so the Doctor asked him if he would be so good as to keep both of them in view.

But some of the silly people, even when they could see the two heads plainly, kept saying that one must be faked. And they would prod the poor timid animal with sticks to see if part of him was stuffed. While two country bumpkins were doing this one day, the pushmi-pullyu got annoyed, and bringing both his heads up sharply at the same time, he jabbed the two inquirers in the leg. Then they knew for sure that he was real and alive all over.

The poor creature had a terrible time those first days. But when Jip told him how much money was being taken in, he was determined to stick it out for John Dolittle's sake. And after a little while, although his opinion of the human race sank very low, he got sort of used to the silly, gaping faces of his audiences, and from both heads, gave them very scornful looks.

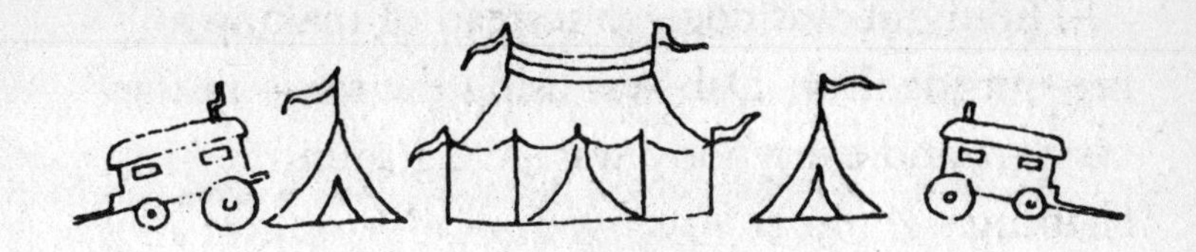

4. *Sophie, from Alaska*

One night on a trip between towns, the procession stopped by the side of the road as usual. Soon after the kettle had been put on to boil, Jip's two new friends, Toby the Punch-and-Judy dog and Swizzle the clown's dog, came to the caravan and joined the Doctor's family.

The night was cool, so instead of making a fire outside, Dab-Dab was using the stove in the caravan, and everybody was sitting round it chatting.

'Have you heard the news, Doctor?' asked Toby, jumping up on the bed.

'No,' said John Dolittle. 'What is it?'

'At the next town - Ashby - we are to pick up Sophie.'

'Who in the world is Sophie?' asked the Doctor, getting out his slippers from behind the stove.

'She left us before you joined,' said Swizzle. 'Sophie's the performing seal - balances balls on her nose and does tricks in the water. She fell sick and Blossom had to leave her behind about a month ago. She's all right now, though, and her keeper is meeting us at Ashby so she can join us again. I'm sure you will like her.'

The circus reached the town of Ashby the next morning. After the tents were all rigged and everything was ready for the afternoon performance, Doctor Dolittle set out to meet the performing seal.

Sophie, a fine five-foot Alaskan seal with sleek skin and intelligent eyes, was one of the features of the big tent twice a day. During the rest of the time she was kept in a tank. Visitors could watch her dive for fish if they paid threepence to come and see her.

When the Doctor arrived at the railing which surrounded the tank, he spoke to her in her own language. Poor Sophie burst into a flood of tears when she realised who the Doctor was.

'What is the matter?' asked John Dolittle.

The seal, still weeping, did not answer.

'Calm yourself,' said the Doctor. 'Don't be hysterical. Tell me, are you still sick? I understood you had recovered.'

'Oh, yes, I got over that,' said Sophie through her tears. 'It was only an upset stomach. They *will* feed us this stale fish, you know.'

'Then what's the matter?' asked the Doctor. 'Why are you crying?'

'I was weeping for joy,' said Sophie. 'I was just thinking as you came in that the only person in the world who could help me in my trouble was John Dolittle. When you first came in I thought you were an ordinary visitor. But the very first word of Sealish that you spoke - and Alaskan Sealish at that - I knew who you were: John Dolittle, the one man in the world I wanted to see! It was too much, I . . .'

'Come, come!' said the Doctor. 'Don't break down again. Tell me what your trouble is.'

'When I was sick they decided I needed company. So they put me in a pond with the other seals until I recovered.' Sophie began to weep again. But she pulled herself together and went on. 'One of the seals who had come from the Bering Strait, as I did, told me that my husband has been unhappy and has refused to eat since I was captured and brought here. He used to be the leader of the herd but he's grown so worried and thin, another seal has been elected in his place. Now my husband isn't expected to live.' Quietly Sophie began to sob. 'I can quite understand it. We were devoted to one another. And although he was so big and strong and no other seal in the herd ever dared to argue with him, without me, well, he is just lost, you know - a mere baby. Poor Slushy! My poor, poor Slushy!'

'Poor who?' asked the Doctor.

'Slushy,' said the seal. 'That's my husband's name. He relied on me for everything - poor, simple Slushy. What shall I do! What shall I do? I ought to go to him.'

'Well, now listen,' said John Dolittle. 'It's not

an easy matter to arrange a trip to Alaska. Perhaps I can persuade Mr Higgins, your keeper, to let you visit - er, Slushy. Cheer up!' he said, leaning over the railing, 'I'll find a way.'

Just then a school teacher with a band of children entered, accompanied by Higgins, the keeper. As Higgins came in, the Doctor went out smiling to himself. Soon the children were laughing with delight at the antics in the tank. And Higgins decided that Sophie must be feeling entirely recovered, for he had never seen her so sprightly or so full of good spirits.

The Doctor returned to the caravan and asked Toby the Punch-and-Judy dog, 'Does Sophie belong to Blossom or to Higgins?'

'To Higgins, Doctor,' said the little dog. 'He does something the same as you do; in return for letting the seal perform in the big ring, Higgins gets his stand in the circus free and pockets whatever money he makes on her as a sideshow.'

'Well, that isn't the same as me at all,' said the Doctor. 'The big difference is that the pushmi-pullyu is here of his own accord and Sophie is kept against her will. It is a perfect scandal that hunters can go up to the Arctic and capture any animals they like, breaking up families and upsetting herd government and community life in this way - a crying shame! Toby, how much does a seal cost?'

'They vary in price, Doctor,' said Toby. 'But I heard Sophie say that when Higgins bought her in Liverpool from the men who had caught her, he paid twenty pounds for her.'

'How much have we got in the money box, Too-Too?' asked the Doctor.

Too-Too, the mathematician, cocked his head on one side and closed his left eye as he always did when calculating.

'Two pounds, five shillings and ninepence, cash in hand, net.'

'Good Lord!' groaned the Doctor, 'barely enough to buy a tenth of Sophie! I wonder if there's anyone I could borrow from.'

'Blossom wouldn't let you buy her even if you had the money,' said Swizzle. 'Higgins is under contract to travel with the circus for a year.'

'Very well, then,' said the Doctor. 'There's only one thing to be done. That seal doesn't belong to those men, anyhow. She's a free citizen of the Arctic Circle. And if she wants to go back there, back she shall go. Sophie must escape.'

5. *Planning the Escape*

Although the plans for Sophie's escape were of course kept a strict secret from any of the people in Blossom's establishment, the animals of the circus soon got to know of them through Jip, Toby and Swizzle.

The plan was for the Doctor to leave the circus a few days ahead of Sophie so that Blossom would not connect her escape with the Doctor. In this way no one would be searching for John Dolittle but would simply be giving chase to an escaped seal.

When John Dolittle returned from announcing to the manager that he was about to leave the circus on business, he found the animals seated about the table in the wagon talking in whispers.

'Well, Doctor,' said Matthew, who was sitting on the steps, 'did you speak to the boss?'

'Yes,' said the Doctor. 'I told him. It's all right.

I'm leaving tonight. I felt frightfully guilty and underhanded. I do wish I could do this openly.'

'You'd stand a fat chance of succeeding, if you did!' said Matthew. 'I don't feel guilty at all.'

'Listen, Doctor,' said Jip. 'Let me know if there's anything I can do to help. When is Sophie going to get away?'

'The day after tomorrow,' said John Dolittle. 'Matthew, here, will undo the door of her stand just after closing time. But listen, Matthew: you'll have to be awfully careful no one sees you tinkering with the lock. If we should get caught we would indeed be in a bad fix then. Do be careful, won't you?'

'You can rely on me, Doctor,' said Matthew, proudly puffing out his chest.

'Get clear out of the way as soon as you have let her free,' said the Doctor, 'so you won't be connected with it at all. Dear me, how like a low-down conspiracy it sounds!'

'Sounds like lots of fun to me,' said Matthew.

'To me, too,' said Jip.

'It'll be the best trick that's been done in this show for a long while,' put in Swizzle. 'Ladies and gentleman: John Dolittle, the world-famous conjurer, will now make a live seal disappear from the stage before your eyes. Abracadabra, mumble-and-jabberer, hoopla, hey presto! Gone!'

And Swizzle stood on his hind legs and bowed to an imaginary audience behind the stove.

'Well,' said the Doctor, 'even though it sounds underhanded, I don't feel I'm doing anything wrong myself. They've no right to keep Sophie in this slavery. How would you and I like it,' he asked Matthew, 'to be made to dive for fish into a tub of dirty water for the amusement of loafers?'

'Rotten!' said Matthew. 'I never did care for fish nor water, neither. But look here, have you arranged with Sophie where she's to meet you?'

'Yes,' said John Dolittle. 'As soon as she gets clear of the circus enclosure - and don't forget we are relying on you to leave the back gate open as well as Sophie's own door - as soon as she's out of the fence, she is to cross the road where she will find an empty house. Alongside of that there is a little dark passage, and in that passage I will be waiting for her. My goodness, I do hope everything goes right! It's so dreadfully important for her - and for all those seals in Alaska, too.'

'And what are you going to do then,' asked Matthew, 'when she's got as far as the passage?'

'Well, it's no use trying to plan too far as to detail. My general idea is to make for the Bristol Channel. Once there, she's all right. But it's nearly a hundred miles as the crow flies; and as we'll have to keep hidden most of the way, I'm not expecting an easy journey. However, I've no doubt we shall get along all right once she's safely away from the circus.'

So that night after a final talk with Sophie, he set out alone - on business. He took with him most of what money he had, leaving a little with Matthew to pay for the small needs of his establishment while he was away. His 'business', as a matter of fact, did not take him further than the next town - which journey he made by stagecoach.

On his arrival at the next town, he took a room in an inn and remained there the whole time. Two nights later he returned to Ashby, after dark, and made his way to his meeting place with Sophie.

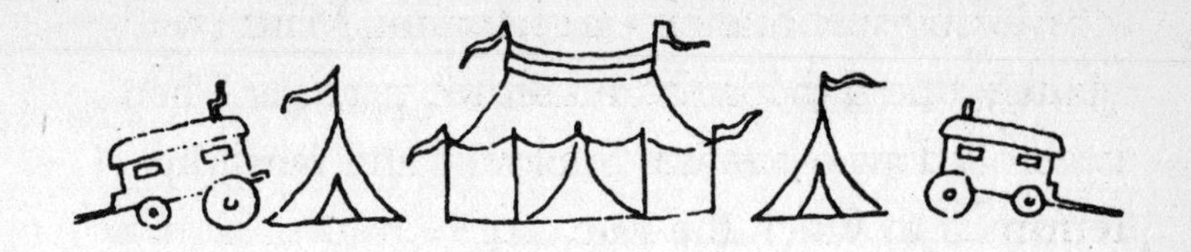

6. The Fun Begins

About ten o'clock, when the circus was beginning to close up, Too-Too stationed himself on top of the menagerie where he could see everything that went on. He had arranged with the elephant and the animals of the collection to start a rumpus in the menagerie on a given signal to attract, if necessary, the attention of the circus men away from the escaping seal. Gub-Gub gave himself the job of watching Blossom, and he took up a post underneath the ringmaster's private caravan.

Well, about an hour after Blossom had locked up the fence gates and retired to his caravan, Matthew slipped away from the pushmi-pullyu's stand and sauntered off across the enclosure. Jip, also pretending he was doing nothing in particular, followed him at a short distance. Everyone seemed to be in bed and Matthew didn't meet a soul as he walked to the gate the Doctor had spoken of.

Making sure that no one saw him, Matthew quickly undid the latch and set the gate ajar. Then he strolled away towards Sophie's stand while Jip remained to watch the gate.

He hadn't been gone more than a minute when along came the circus watchman with a lantern. He closed the gate, and, to Jip's horror, locked it with a key. Jip, still pretending he was just sniffing around the fence after rats, waited till the man had disappeared again. Then he raced off towards Sophie's stand to find Matthew.

Now things had not turned out for Matthew as easy as he had expected. On approaching the seal's tank house, he had seen Higgins sitting on the steps smoking and looking at the moon. Matthew therefore hid in the shadow of a tent and waited for the seal's keeper to go to bed.

Higgins, he knew, slept in a wagon close to Blossom's on the other side of the enclosure. But while he watched and waited, instead of Higgins going away, the watchman came over to join him, sat down on the steps and started chatting.

Presently, Jip, smelling out Matthew behind the tent, came up and tried frantically to make him understand that the gate he had opened had been closed again and locked. Jip had very little success in trying to make Matthew understand him, and for nearly an hour Matthew stayed in the shadow waiting for the two figures on the steps of Sophie's stand to move away and leave the coast clear for him to let the seal free.

In the meantime, John Dolittle in his narrow, dark passage outside the circus enclosure wondered what the delay was and tried to read his watch by the dim light of the moon.

Finally, Matthew decided that the two men were never going to bed. So, swearing under his breath, he crept away from the shadow of the tent and set off to find Theodosia, his wife.

On arrival at his own wagon, he found her darning socks by the light of the candle.

'Pst! Theodosia,' he whispered through the window. 'Listen.'

'Good Lord!' gasped Mrs Mugg, dropping her needlework. 'What a fright you gave me, Matthew! Is it all right? Has the seal got away?'

'No, it's all wrong. Higgins and the watchman are sitting on the steps talking. I can't get near the door while they're there. Go up and draw 'em off for me, will yer? Tell 'em a tent's blown down or something - anything to get 'em away.'

'All right,' said Theodosia. 'Wait till I get my shawl. I'll bring them over here for some cocoa.'

Then the helpful Mrs Mugg went off and invited Higgins and the watchman to come to her husband's wagon for a little party. Matthew would be along to join them presently, she said.

As soon as the coast was clear, Matthew sped up the steps of the seal's stand and, in a minute, his nimble fingers had the door unlocked. Just

inside lay Sophie, all ready to start out upon her long journey. With a grunt of thanks she waddled forth into the moonlight, slid down the steps and set off clumsily towards the gate.

Once more Jip tried his hardest to make Matthew understand that something was wrong. But Matthew merely took the dog's signals of distress for joy and marched off to join his wife's cocoa party, feeling that his share of the night's work had been well done.

In the meantime, Sophie had waddled her way laboriously to the gate and found it locked. Jip then searched all around the fence, trying to find a hole big enough for her to get through. But he couldn't find one. Poor Sophie had escaped the captivity of her tank only to find herself still a prisoner within the circus enclosure.

Everything that had happened up to this point had been carefully watched by a little round bird perched on the roof of the menagerie. Too-Too, the listener, the night seer, the mathematician, was more than usually wide-awake. And presently, while Jip was still nosing around the fence trying to find Sophie a way out, he heard the whir of wings over his head and an owl alighted by his side.

'For heaven's sake, Jip,' whispered Too-Too, 'keep your head. The game will be up if you don't. You're doing no good by running around like that. Get Sophie into hiding. Look at her, lying out in the moonlight there, as though this were Greenland! If anyone should come along and see her we're lost. Hide her until Matthew sees what has happened to the gate. Hurry - I see someone coming.'

As Too-Too flew back to his place on the menagerie roof, Jip rushed off to Sophie and in a few hurried words explained the situation to her.

'Come over here,' he said. 'Get in this tent. So! Gosh! Only just in time! There's the light of a lantern moving. Now lie perfectly still and wait till I come and tell you.'

And in his little dark passage beyond the circus fence, John Dolittle once more looked at his watch and muttered, 'What can have happened? Will she never come?'

It was not many minutes after Matthew had joined the cocoa party in his own wagon that the watchman rose from the table and said he ought to be getting along on his rounds. Matthew, anxious to give Sophie as much time as possible to get away, tried to persuade him to stay.

'Oh, stop and have another cup of cocoa!' he said.

'No,' said the watchman, 'thank ye. I'd like to, but I mustn't. Blossom gave me strict orders to keep movin' the whole night. If he was to come and not find me on the job, I'd catch it hot.'

And in spite of everything Matthew could do to keep him, the watchman took his lamp and left.

Higgins, however, remained. And while Matthew and his wife talked to him, they expected any moment to hear a shout outside warning the circus that Sophie had escaped.

But the watchman, when he found the stand open and empty, did not begin by shouting. He came running back to Matthew's wagon.

'Higgins,' he yelled, 'your seal's gone!'

'Gone!' cried Higgins.

'Gone!' said Matthew. 'Can't be possible!'

'I tell you she 'as,' said the watchman. ''Er door's open and she ain't there.'

'Good heavens!' cried Higgins, springing up. 'I could swear I locked the door as usual. But if the gates in the fence was all closed, she can't be far away. We can soon find 'er again. Come on!'

And he ran out of the wagon with Matthew and Theodosia, pretending to be greatly disturbed, close at his heels.

'I'll go take another look at the gates,' said the watchman. 'I'm sure they're all right. But I'll make double certain anyway.'

Then Higgins, Matthew and Theodosia raced off for the seal's stand.

'The door's open, sure enough,' said Matthew as they came up to it. ''Ow very peculiar!'

'Let's go inside,' said Higgins. 'Maybe she's hiding at the bottom of the tank.'

Then all three of them went in and by the light of matches peered down into the dark water.

Meanwhile, the watchman turned up again. 'The gates are all right,' he said. 'Closed and locked, every one of them.'

Then at last Matthew knew something had gone wrong. And while Higgins and the watchman were examining the water with the lamp, he whispered something to his wife, slipped out and ran for the gate, hoping Theodosia would keep the other two at the stand long enough for him to sort things out.

As a matter of fact she played her part very well, did Mrs Mugg. Presently Higgins said, 'There ain't nothing under the water. Sophie's not here. Let's go outside and look for her.'

Then just as the two men turned to leave, Theodosia cried, 'What's that?'

'What's what?' said Higgins, turning back.

'That - down there,' said Mrs Mugg, pointing into the dirty water. 'I thought I saw something move. Bring the lantern nearer.'

The watchman crouched over the edge of the tank, and Higgins, beside him, screwed up his eyes to see better.

'I don't see nothing,' said the keeper.

'Oh! Oh! I'm feeling faint!' cried Mrs Mugg. 'Help me. I'm going to fall in!'

And Theodosia, a heavy woman, swayed and suddenly crumpled up on top of the two crouching men.

Then, splash! splash! in fell, not Theodosia, but Higgins and the watchman – lamp and all.

7. *'Animals' Night' at the Circus*

That was one of the busiest and jolliest nights the circus ever had - from the animals' point of view; and the two men falling in the water and yelling for help was the beginning of a grand racket which finally woke the whole town.

First of all, Blossom, hearing the noise, came rushing out of his caravan. At the foot of the steps a pig appeared from nowhere, rushed between his legs, and tripped him up. Throughout the whole proceedings, Gub-Gub kept popping out from behind something and upsetting Blossom.

Next, Fatima, the snake charmer, ran from her caravan with a candle in one hand and a hammer in the other. She hadn't gone two steps before a mysterious duck flew over her head and, with one sweep of its wing, blew the candle out. Fatima ran back, relit the candle, and tried again to go to the rescue. But the same thing happened. Dab-Dab kept Fatima almost as busy as Gub-Gub kept Blossom.

Then Mrs Blossom, hastily putting on her dressing gown, appeared upon the scene. She was met by the old horse Beppo. She tried to get by him and Beppo moved out of her way. But in doing so he trod on her corns so badly that she went howling back to bed again and did not reappear.

But although the animals managed by various tricks to keep many people occupied, they could not attend to all the circus folk; and before long the watchman and Higgins, yelling murder in the tank, had attracted a whole lot of tent riggers and other showmen to Sophie's stand.

Now, in the meantime, Matthew Mugg had re-opened the gate in the fence. But when he looked around for Sophie she was nowhere to be seen. Jip and Too-Too, as a matter of fact, were the only ones who really knew where she was. Jip, however, with all this crowd of men rushing around the seal's stand near the gate, was afraid to give Sophie the word to leave her hiding place. Everybody was shouting, one half asking what the matter was, the other half telling them. Mr Blossom, after being thrown down in the mud by Gub-Gub for the sixth time, was hitting everyone he met and bellowing like a mad bull. The hubbub and confusion were awful.

At last Higgins and the watchman were fished out of their bathtub and, highly perfumed with fish, they joined the hunt.

The watchman and everyone were sure that Sophie must be somewhere near - which was quite true: the tent she was in was only thirty feet from her stand, but the gate she was to escape through was also quite near.

While Jip was wondering when the men would move away so he could let her go, Higgins cried out that he had found a track in the soft earth. Then a dozen lanterns were brought forward and the men started to follow the trail that Sophie had left behind on the way to her hiding place.

Luckily, with so many feet crossing and recrossing the same part of the enclosure, the flipper marks were not easy to make out. Nevertheless, even with Matthew doing his best to lead them off on a wrong scent, the trackers steadily moved in the right direction - towards the tent where poor Sophie, the devoted wife, lay in hiding with a beating heart. Closer and closer the trackers came towards the spot where Jip had hidden the seal. The poor dog was in despair.

However, he had forgotten Too-Too the mathematician. From his lookout on the menagerie roof, away off on the far side of the enclosure, the little owl was still surveying the battlefield with a general's eye. He was waiting only till he was sure that all the circus folk had left their beds to join the hunt and that there were no more to come. When he played his masterstroke of strategy he did not want any extra interference from unexpected quarters.

Suddenly he flew down to a ventilator in the menagerie wall and hooted softly. At his signal there began within the most terrible pandemonium that was ever heard. The lion roared, the yak bellowed, the hyena howled and the elephant trumpeted and stamped his enormous feet. It was the grand climax to the animals' conspiracy.

On the other side of the enclosure the trackers and hunters stood still and listened.

'What in thunder's that?' asked Blossom.

'Coming from the menagerie, ain't it?' said one of the men. 'Sounds like the elephant's broke loose.'

'I know,' said another. 'It's Sophie. She's got into the menagerie and scared the elephant.'

'That's it,' said Blossom. 'Lord, and us huntin' for 'er over here! To the menagerie!' And he grabbed up a lantern and started to run.

'To the menagerie!' yelled the crowd. And in

a moment, to Jip's delight, they were all gone, rushing away to the other side of the enclosure.

All but one. Matthew Mugg, hanging back, pretending to do up his shoelace, saw Jip flash across to a small tent and disappear under the skirt.

'Now,' said Jip. 'Run, Sophie! Swim! Fly! Anything! Get out of the gate!'

Hopping and flopping, Sophie covered the ground as best she could, while Jip yelped to her to hurry and Matthew held the gate open. At last the seal waddled out on to the road and Matthew saw her cross it and disappear into the passage alongside the deserted house. He closed the gate again and stamped out her tracks at the foot of it. Then he leaned against it, mopping his brow.

'Holy smoke!' he sighed. 'And I told the Doctor I done worse things than help a seal escape!'

8. *Free at Last?*

And so at last John Dolittle, waiting, anxious and impatient in the dark passage alongside the empty house, heard to his delight the sound of a peculiar footstep. A flipper-step, it should more properly be called; for the noise of Sophie travelling over a pavement was a strange mixture between someone slapping the ground with a wet rag and a sack of potatoes being yanked along a floor.

'Is that you, Sophie?' he whispered.

'Yes,' said the seal, hitching herself forward to where the Doctor stood.

'Thank goodness! What in the world kept you so long?'

'Oh, there was some mix-up with the gates,' said Sophie. 'But hadn't we better be getting out of the town? It doesn't seem very safe here to me.'

'There's no chance of that for the moment,'

said the Doctor. 'The noise they made in the circus has woken everybody. We dare not try and get through the streets now.'

'But then what are we going to do?'

'We'll have to stay here for a while. It would be madness to try and run for it now.'

'Well, but suppose they come searching in here. We couldn't . . .'

At that moment two people with lanterns stopped at the end of the passage, talked a moment, and moved away.

'Quite so,' whispered the Doctor. 'This isn't safe either. We must find a better place.'

Now, on one side of this alleyway there was a high stone wall, and on the other a high brick wall. The brick wall enclosed the back garden belonging to the deserted house.

'If we could only get into that old empty house,' murmured the Doctor. 'We'd be safe to stay there as long as we wished till this excitement among the townsfolk dies down. Can you think of any way you could get over that wall?'

The seal measured the height with her eye. 'Eight feet,' she murmured. 'I could do it with a ladder. I've been trained to walk up ladders. I do it in the circus, you know. Perhaps . . .'

'Sh!' whispered the Doctor. Listen, there's just a chance I may find an orchard ladder in the garden. Now you wait here; lie flat and wait till I come back.'

Then John Dolittle, a very active man in spite of his round figure, drew back and took a running jump at the wall. His fingers caught the top of it; he hauled himself up, threw one leg over and dropped lightly down into a flower bed on the other side. At the bottom of the garden he saw a toolshed. Slipping up to the door, he opened it and lit a match.

And there, sure enough, hanging against the wall was a ladder. In a moment he had blown out the match and was marching down the garden with the ladder on his shoulder.

Standing it in a firm place, he scaled up and sat on the wall. Next he pulled the ladder up after him and lowered the foot end into the passage.

Then John Dolittle, perched astride the top of the wall (looking exactly like Humpty Dumpty), whispered down into the dark passage below him, 'Now climb up, Sophie. I'll keep this end steady. And when you reach the top get on to the wall beside me till I change the ladder over to the garden side. Easy does it.'

It was a good thing that Sophie was so well trained in balancing. Never in the circus had she performed a better trick than she did that night. It was a feat that even a person might well be proud of. But she knew that her freedom and the happiness of her husband depended on her steadiness. And though she was in constant fear that any minute someone might come down the passage and discover them, it gave her a real thrill to turn the tables on her captors by using the skill they had taught her to escape them.

Firmly, rung by rung, she began hoisting her heavy body upward. Fortunately the ladder was longer than the height of the wall so the Doctor had been able to set it at an easier, flattish slope instead of straight upright. Then, once Sophie had reached the top, she had to shift her clumsy bulk on to the wall.

Fortunately, Sophie had been trained to balance herself on small spaces, as well as to climb ladders, in the circus. And after the Doctor had helped her by leaning down and hoisting her up, she wiggled herself along the top of the wall beside him and kept her balance as easily as though it were nothing at all.

Then, while Sophie gave a fine imitation of a statue in the moonlight, the Doctor hauled the ladder up after her, swung it and lowered it into the garden once more.

Coming down, Sophie did another of her show tricks: she laid herself across the ladder and slid to the bottom. It was quicker than climbing.

'Do you think we'll be able to get away soon,

Doctor?' asked Sophie. 'I'm very anxious to get started.'

'I hope so,' said the Doctor. 'But we must wait until things get quieter. Try and be patient.'

About half an hour later the Doctor took the ladder and, mounting near the top of the garden wall, he listened long and carefully.

'There are still an awful lot of people moving about in the streets,' he said. 'But whether they are circus men hunting you, or just ordinary townsfolk walking about, I can't make out. We'd better wait a while longer, I think.'

'Oh, dear!' sighed Sophie. 'Are we never going to get further than this garden? Poor Slushy! I'm so worried.' And she began to weep softly.

After another hour had gone by, the Doctor went out again. This time, just as he was about to climb the ladder, he heard Jip whispering to him on the other side of the wall.

'Doctor, are you there?'

'Yes, what is it?'

'Listen! Higgins and the boss have gone off somewhere with a wagon. Too-Too thinks it's a grand chance for you to make a dash for it and get out of the town. Have you got that?'

'Yes, I heard you. Thank you, Jip. All right. We'll leave in fifteen minutes.' And the Doctor looked at his watch. 'Which way did Blossom go?'

'East - towards Grimbledon. Swizzle followed them and came back and told us. You make for the west. Can you hear me?'

'Yes, I understand,' whispered the Doctor. Then he told Sophie to be ready. 'Now, listen,' said the Doctor. 'If we meet anyone on the street - and we are pretty sure to - you lie down by the wall and pretend you're a sack I'm carrying and that I'm taking a rest, you see. Understand?'

'All right,' said Sophie. 'I'm frightfully excited. See how my flippers are fluttering.'

Well, the Doctor kept an eye on his watch and after fifteen minutes he whispered, 'All right, I think we can start now. Let me go first so I can steady the ladder for you, the way I did before.'

But alas for poor Sophie's hopes! Just as the Doctor was halfway up, the noise of distant barking, deep-voiced and angry, broke out.

John Dolittle paused on the ladder, frowning. The barking of many dogs together, drew nearer.

'What's that?' said Sophie in a tremulous whisper from below. 'That's not Jip or any of our dogs.'

'No,' said the Doctor, climbing down slowly. 'There's no mistaking that sound. Sophie, something's gone wrong. That's the baying of bloodhounds – bloodhounds on a scent. And they're coming this way!'

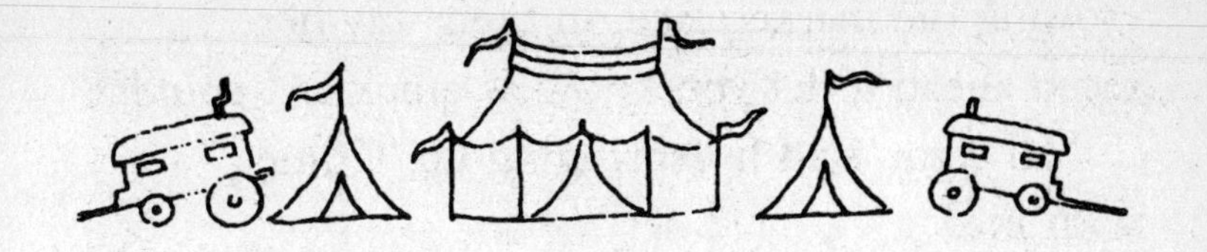

9. The Bloodhounds

Jip, after his last conversation with the Doctor over the garden wall, returned to the caravan and his friends, feeling comfortably sure that everything would go all right now.

He and Too-Too were chatting under the table while Dab-Dab was dusting the furniture, when suddenly in rushed Toby, all out of breath.

'Jip,' he cried. 'The worst has happened! They've got bloodhounds. That's what Blossom and Higgins went off for. They're bringing 'em here in a wagon - six of 'em. I spotted them just as they entered the town over the tollbridge. I ran behind and tried to speak to the dogs. But with the rattle of the wagon wheels they couldn't hear me. If they put those hounds on Sophie's trail she's as good as caught already.'

'Confound them!' muttered Jip. 'Where are they now, Toby?'

'I don't know. When I left them they were

crossing the marketplace on their way here. I raced ahead to let you know as quick as I could.'

'All right,' said Jip, springing up. 'Come with me.'

And he dashed out into the night.

'They'll try and pick up the trail from the seal's stand,' said Jip as the two dogs ran on together across the enclosure. 'Perhaps we can meet them there.'

But at the stand there were no bloodhounds.

Jip put his nose to the ground and sniffed just once. 'Drat the luck!' he whispered. 'They've been here already and gone off on the trail. Listen, there they are, baying now. Come on! Let's race for the passage. We may be in time yet.'

And away he sped while poor little Toby, left far behind with his flappy ears trailing in the wind, put on his best speed to keep up.

Dashing into the passage, Jip found it full of men and dogs and lanterns. Blossom was there, and Higgins, and the man who owned the hounds. While the men talked and waved the lamps, the hounds, six great, droopy-jowled beasts with long ears and bloodshot eyes, sniffed the ground and ran hither and thither about the alley, trying to find where the trail led out. Every once in a while they would lift their noses, open their big mouths, and send a deep-voiced howl rolling towards the moon.

Jip ran into the crowded passage, pretending to join in the hunt for a scent. Picking out the biggest bloodhound, who, he guessed, was the leader, he got alongside him. Then, still keeping his eyes and nose to the ground, he whispered in dog language, 'Get your duffers out of here. This is the Doctor's business - John Dolittle's.'

The bloodhound paused and eyed Jip haughtily. 'Who are you, mongrel?' he said. 'We've been set to run down a seal. Stop trying to fool us. John Dolittle is away on a voyage.'

'He's nothing of the kind,' muttered Jip. 'He's on the other side of that wall - not six feet away from us. He is trying to get this seal down to the sea so she can escape these men with the lanterns - if you idiots will only get out of the way.'

'I don't believe you,' said the leader. 'The last I heard of the Doctor he was travelling in Africa. We must do our duty.'

'Duffer! Numbskull!' growled Jip, losing his temper entirely. 'I'm telling you the truth. For two pins I'd pull your long ears. The Doctor's been back in England over a month. He's travelling with the circus now.'

But the leader of the bloodhounds was very obstinate and a bit stupid. He would not believe that the Doctor wasn't still abroad. In all his famous record as a tracker, he had never failed to run down his quarry once he took up a scent. He had a big reputation, and was proud of it. He wasn't going to be misled by every whippersnapper of a dog who came along with an idle tale - no, not he.

Poor Jip was in despair. He saw that the hounds were now sniffing at the wall over which Sophie had climbed. He knew that these great beasts would never leave this neighbourhood while the seal was near and her fishy scent so strong all about. It was only a matter of time before Blossom and Higgins would guess that she was in hiding beyond the wall and would have the old house and garden searched.

While he was still arguing, an idea came to Jip. He left the knot of bloodhounds and nosed his way carelessly down to the bottom of the passage. The air was now simply full of barks and yelps from dogs of every kind. Jip threw back his head and pretended to join in the chorus. But the message he shouted was directed over the wall to the Doctor: 'These idiots won't believe me. For heaven's sake tell 'em you're here - Woof! Woof! WOO–'

And then still another doggish voice, coming from the garden, added to the general noise of the night. And this is what it barked: 'It is I, John Dolittle. Won't you please go away! Wow! Woof! Wow-ow!'

At the sound of that voice - to Blossom and Higgins no different from any of the other yelps that filled the air - the noses of all six bloodhounds left the ground and twelve long ears cocked up, motionless and listening.

'By ginger!' muttered the leader. 'It is he! It's the great man himself!'

'What did I tell you?' whispered Jip, shuffling towards him. 'Now lead these men off towards the south - out of the town, quick - and don't stop running till morning.'

Then the dog trainer saw his prize leader suddenly double round and head out of the passage. To his delight, the others followed his example.

'All right, Mr Blossom,' he yelled, waving his lantern. 'They've got the scent again. Come on, follow 'em, follow 'em! They're going fast. Stick to 'em! Run!'

Tumbling over one another to keep up, the three men hurried after the hounds.

'They've turned down the street to the south,' shouted the owner. 'We'll get your seal now, never fear. Ah, they're good dogs! Once they take the scent they never go wrong. Come on, Mr Blossom. Don't let 'em get too far away.'

And in a flash the little dark passage, which a moment before was full and crowded, was left empty in the moonlight.

Poor Sophie, weeping hysterically on the lawn with the Doctor trying to comfort her, suddenly saw the figure of an owl pop up on to the garden wall.

'Doctor! Doctor!'

'Yes, Too-Too. What is it?'

'Now's your chance! The whole town's joined the hunt. Get your ladder. Hurry!'

And two minutes later, while the hounds, in full cry, led Blossom and Higgins on a grand steeplechase over hill and dale, the Doctor led Sophie quietly out of Ashby, towards the sea.

10. *Sophie in Disguise*

Sophie and John Dolittle plodded along the road between the hedgerows in the dark. Sophie's heavy and slow pace told the Doctor that even this bit of land travel was tiring the poor beast. Yet he dared not stop on the highway.

Arriving at a little clump of brambles and trees, they decided it would make a good, snug place in which to take a rest. It was the kind of place where no one would be likely to come in a month of Sundays - except perhaps children berry-picking.

'Well,' said the Doctor, as Sophie flopped down, panting, within the protection of dense hawthorns and furze, 'so far, so good!'

'My!' said Sophie, 'but I'm winded. Seals weren't meant for this kind of thing, Doctor. How far do you reckon we've come?'

'About a mile and a half, I should say.'

'Good Lord! Is that all? And it's nearly a

hundred to the sea! Oh, Doctor,' sobbed Sophie, 'I'm too weary to go any further.' She flopped on the grass and wept.

'Now, now, Sophie,' said the Doctor, patting her on the head. 'You leave it to me. We'll rest the night here and in the morning I'll go to the nearby town and get us some food. You'll feel better then, let's make the best of it and rest now.'

Next morning the Doctor set out, leaving

Sophie still asleep. After a walk of about two miles, he came to a village with a pretty little ivy-covered inn called The Three Huntsmen. Going in he ordered breakfast. A very old waiter served him some bacon and eggs.

As soon as the Doctor had eaten, he lit his pipe and began chatting to the waiter. He found out a whole lot of things about the coaches that ran up and down the Grantchester Road - what the different ones were like to look at, at what hour they were to be expected, which of them were usually crowded, and much more.

Then he left the inn and walked down the street till he came to the few shops the village had. One of these was a general clothes shop. The Doctor entered and asked the price of a lady's cloak that was hanging in the window.

'Fifteen shillings and sixpence,' said the woman in charge of the shop. 'Is your wife tall?'

'My wife?' asked the Doctor, entirely bewildered. 'Oh, ah, yes, of course. Well - er - I want it long anyway. And I'll take a bonnet, too. And now I want a lady's veil - a heavy one, please.'

'Oh, mourning in the family?'

'Er - not exactly. But I want it pretty thick - a travelling veil.'

Then the woman added a veil to the Doctor's purchases. And with a large parcel under his arm he presently left the shop. Next, he went to a grocery and bought some dried herrings for Sophie, and about noon he started back down the road.

'Sophie,' said John Dolittle, when he reached the seal's hiding place in the woods, 'I have a whole lot of information for you, some food, and some clothes.'

'Some clothes!' said Sophie. 'What would I do with clothes?'

'Wear them,' said the Doctor. 'You've got to be a lady - for a while, anyhow.'

'Great heavens!' grunted Sophie, wiping her whiskers with the back of her flipper. 'What for?'

'So you can travel by coach,' said the Doctor.

'But I can't walk upright,' cried Sophie, 'like a lady.'

'I know. But you can sit upright - like a sick lady. You'll have to be a little lame. Any walking there is to be done, I'll carry you.'

'But what about my face? It isn't the right shape.'

'We'll cover that up with a veil,' said the Doctor, 'and your hat will disguise the rest of your head. Now, eat this fish I've brought for you and then we will rehearse dressing you up.'

Then the Doctor dressed up Sophie, the performing seal, like a lady. He seated her on a log, put the bonnet on her head, the veil across her face, and the cloak over the rest of her.

After he had got her into a human sitting position on the log, it was surprising how natural she looked. In the deep hood of the bonnet, her long nose was entirely concealed;

and with the veil hung over the front of it, her head looked extraordinarily like a woman's.

'How am I supposed to breathe?' asked Sophie, blowing out the veil in front like a balloon.

'Don't do that,' said the Doctor. 'You're not swimming or coming up for air. You'll get used to it after a while.'

'I can't keep very steady this way, Doctor. I'm sitting on the back of my spine, you know. It's an awfully hard position for balancing - much worse than walking on a ladder. What if I should slip down on to the floor of the coach?'

'The seat will be wider than this log and more comfortable. Besides, I'll try to get you into a corner and I'll sit close beside you so you'll be sort of wedged in. If you feel yourself slipping, just whisper to me and I'll hitch you up into a safer position. You look splendid - really, you do.'

When evening came it found Doctor Dolittle by the edge of the road, with a heavily veiled woman seated at his side, waiting for the Grantchester coach.

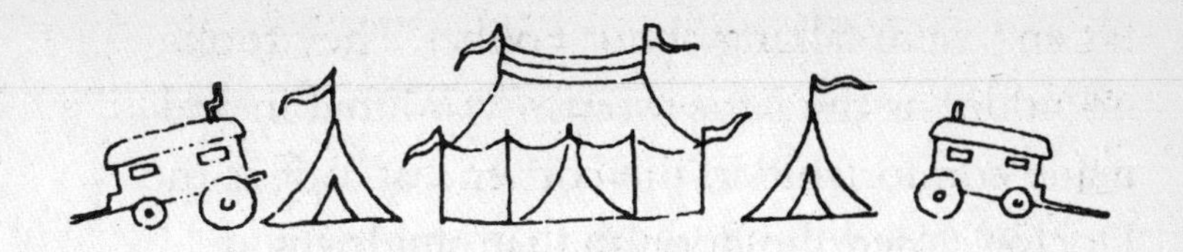

11. *The Grantchester Coach*

After they had waited about a quarter of an hour, Sophie said, 'I hear wheels, Doctor. And look, there are the lights, far down the road.'

'Ah!' said the Doctor. 'That's ours all right. Now sit up by the side of the road here and keep perfectly still till I signal the driver. Then I'll lift you in. Is your bonnet on tight?'

'Yes,' said Sophie. 'But the veil is tickling my nose most awfully. I do hope I don't sneeze.'

'So do I,' said the Doctor, remembering the cow-like bellow that seals make when they sneeze.

Then John Dolittle stepped out into the middle of the road and stopped the coach. Inside he found three passengers - two men at the far end and an old lady near the door. To his delight, the corner seat opposite the old lady was empty.

Leaving the door open, he ran back and carried Sophie to the coach. The two men at the far end were talking about politics. They took no notice as the lame woman was lifted in and made comfortable in the corner seat. But as the Doctor closed the door and sat beside his companion, he noticed that the old lady opposite was very interested in his invalid.

The coach started off, and the Doctor, after making sure that Sophie's flippers were not showing below the cape, got out a newspaper from his pocket and pretended to be deeply absorbed in it.

Presently the old lady leaned forward and tapped Sophie on the knee.

'Excuse me, my dear . . .' she began in a kindly voice.

'Oh, er . . .' said the Doctor, looking up quickly. 'She doesn't talk - er - that is, not any English.'

'Has she got far to go?' asked the old lady.

'To Alaska,' said the Doctor, forgetting himself, 'er - that is, eventually. This journey, we're only going to Grantchester.'

Wishing people would mind their own business, the Doctor plunged again into his paper as though his life depended on his reading every word.

But the kindly passenger was not easily put off. After a moment she leaned forward once more and tapped the Doctor on the knee.

'Is it rheumatics?' she asked in a whisper, nodding towards Sophie. 'I noticed that you had to carry her in, poor dear!'

'Er, not exactly,' stammered the Doctor. 'Her legs are too short. Can't walk a step. Been that way all her life.'

'Dear me!' sighed the old lady. 'How sad; how very sad! She'll be your daughter, I suppose?' asked the old lady.

But this time Sophie spoke for herself. A deep roar suddenly shook the carriage. The tickling of the veil had finally made her sneeze. And before the Doctor could avoid it, she slid down on to the floor between his feet.

'She's in pain, poor thing,' said the old lady. 'Wait till I get out my smelling bottle. She's fainted. I often do it myself, travelling. And this coach does smell something horrible - fishy like.'

Luckily for the Doctor, the old lady then busied herself hunting in her handbag. He was therefore able, while lifting the seal back on to the seat, to place himself in between Sophie and the two men, who were now also showing interest in her.

'Here you are,' said the old lady, handing out a silver smelling bottle. 'Lift up her veil and hold it under her nose.'

'No, thank you,' said the Doctor quickly. 'All she needs is rest. She's very tired. We'll prop her up snugly in the corner, like this - so. Now, let's not talk, and probably she'll soon drop off to sleep.'

The two men continued glancing in Sophie's

direction and talking in whispers in a way that made the Doctor very uneasy.

Eventually the coach stopped to change horses at the village of Shottlake. The driver told the passengers that if they wished to have supper at the inn, they had half an hour to do so.

The two men left the coach, eyeing Sophie and the Doctor as they passed on their way out; and soon the old lady followed their example. The driver had now also disappeared and John Dolittle and his companion had the coach to themselves.

'Listen, Sophie,' the Doctor whispered. 'I'm getting uneasy about those two men. I'm afraid they suspect that you are not what you pretend to be. You stay here now, while I go in and find out if they're travelling any further with us.'

Then he strolled into the inn. In the passage he met a serving maid. 'Pardon me,' he began. 'Do you happen to know who those two men were who came in off the coach just now?'

'Yes, sir,' said the maid. 'One of them's the County Constable and the other's Mr Tuttle, the mayor of Penchurch.'

'Thank you,' said the Doctor, and passed on.

Reaching the screen door, he hesitated a

moment before entering the dining room. And presently he heard the voices of the two men seated at a table on the other side of the screen.

'I tell you,' said the one in a low tone, 'there's not the least doubt. They're highwaymen, as sure as you're alive. It's an old trick, disguising as a woman. Did you notice the thick veil? As likely as not it's that rogue, Robert Finch himself. He robbed the Twinborough Express only last month.'

'I shouldn't wonder,' said the other. 'And the short, thick villain will be Joe Gresham, his partner. Now, I'll tell you what we'll do - after supper let's go back and take our seats as though we suspected nothing. Their plan, no doubt, is to wait till the coach is full and has reached a lonely part of the road. Then they'll hold up the passengers - money or your life! - and get away before the alarm can be raised. Have you got your travelling pistols?'

'Yes.'

'All right, give me one. Now, when I nudge you - you tear off the man's veil and hold a pistol to his head. I'll take care of the short one. Then we'll turn the coach about, drive back, and lodge them in the village jail. Understand?'

Without waiting to have supper, the Doctor left the inn and sped across the yard to the coach.

'Sophie,' he whispered, 'come out of there. They think we're highwaymen in disguise. Let's get away! Quick! While the coast is clear.'

Hoisting the seal's huge weight in his arms, the Doctor staggered out of the yard, across the road, and into the ditch on the other side. He put her down.

'Give me your cloak and bonnet - that's it.

Now you can travel better.'

A few minutes later they were safe behind a high hedge, resting in the long, sweet grass of a meadow.

'My!' sighed Sophie, stretching herself out. 'It's good to be rid of that wretched cloak and veil. I don't like being a lady one bit. And as for coaches – I'd rather swim.'

'I'm sure you would,' said the Doctor. 'But, thank goodness, we're much farther on our way.'

'How long to the Bristol Channel now?' asked Sophie.

'Well,' began the Doctor, 'I'm not too sure, but I think about two days – walking.'

'Walking?' cried Sophie. 'I can't walk it, Doctor, I simply can't. Not two whole days.'

'S-h-h!' whispered John Dolittle. 'I think I hear something moving beyond the hedge.'

Whoever it was, he seemed determined to enter the field at that point. So with a whispered word to Sophie, the Doctor sprang up and started running across the meadow, with the poor seal flopping along at his side.

On and on they went. Behind them they heard heavy footsteps beating the ground in pursuit.

Presently the Doctor, knowing that they were losing the race, turned to look back. And there, lumbering along behind them, was an old, old plough horse!

'It's all right, Sophie,' panted the Doctor halting. 'It isn't a man at all. We've had our run for nothing. Good lord, but I'm blown!'

The horse, seeing them stop, slowed down to a walk and came ambling towards them in the moonlight.

'Heavens!' cried the Doctor. 'It's my old friend from Puddleby. Why didn't you call to me instead of chasing us across country?

'Is that John Dolittle's voice I hear?' asked the old horse, peering close into the Doctor's face.

'Yes,' said the Doctor. 'And I'm very glad to see you.'

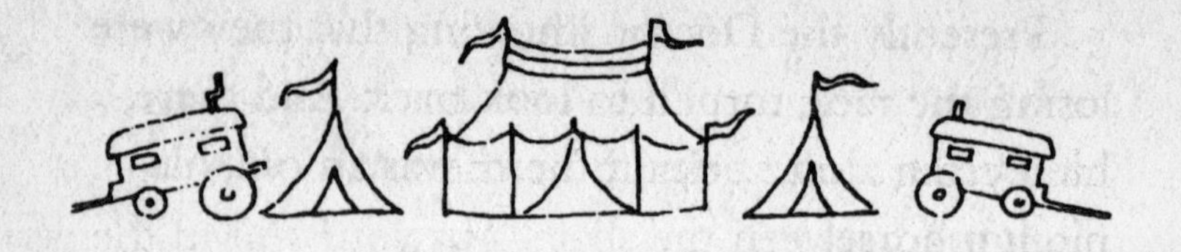

12. Old Friends and New

'Is he a nice man, this farmer you're working for now?' asked the Doctor several minutes later as he seated himself in the grass of the meadow.

'Oh, yes,' said the old horse. 'He means well. But I haven't done much work this year. He's got a younger team for ploughing. I'm sort of pensioned off - only do odd jobs. But what's this animal you have with you,' asked the short-sighted plough horse as Sophie moved restlessly in the grass, 'a badger?'

'No, that's a seal. Let me introduce you: this is Sophie, from Alaska. We're escaping from the circus. She has to go back to her country on urgent business, and I'm helping her get to the Bristol Channel. From there she can swim to the sea and in a few days - at her swimming speed - she should get to Alaska in record time.'

'Perhaps I can help,' said the old horse. 'Listen,

you see that barn up on the skyline? Well, there's an old wagon in it. There's no harness but there's plenty of ropes. Let's run up there, and you can hitch me between the shafts, put your seal in the wagon, and we'll go.'

'But you'll get into trouble,' said the Doctor, 'taking your farmer's wagon off like that.'

'My farmer will never know,' said the old horse, grinning. 'You leave the gate on the latch as we go out, and I'll bring the wagon back and put it where we found it.'

'But how will you get out of your harness alone?'

'That's easy. If you knot the ropes the way I tell you, I can undo them with my teeth. I won't be able to take you the whole way because I couldn't get back in time to put the wagon away before the daylight comes. But I've got a friend about fifteen miles down the Grantchester Road, on the Redhill Farm. He gets put out to graze at night, like me. He'll take you the rest of the way. It'll be easy for him to get back to his place before anyone's about.'

'Old friend,' said the Doctor, 'you have a great head. Let's hurry and get on our way.'

They climbed the hill to the barn. John

Dolittle hitched up the horse, being careful to make all the knots exactly the way he was told. Then lifting Sophie into the wagon, they started off down the meadow towards the gate.

As they were driving out, the Doctor said, 'But suppose anyone should meet me driving a wagon in a high hat? Wouldn't it seem sort of suspicious? Oh, look: there's a scarecrow in the next field. I'll borrow *his* hat.'

'Bring the whole scarecrow with you,' the old

horse called after him as the Doctor started off. 'I'll need something as a dummy driver when I'm coming back. Folks would stop me if they thought I was straying around the country without a driver.'

'All right,' said the Doctor and he ran off.

In a few minutes he came marching back with the scarecrow on his shoulder. Then he set the gate on the latch so the old horse could push it open on his return, threw the scarecrow up into the wagon, and climbed in himself.

Next, he took the scarecrow's tattered hat and put it on his own head, in the place of his high one. Then he got into the driver's seat, lifted the rope reins in his hands, called 'Gee-up!' to his old friend between the shafts, and they started off.

'You'd better keep your cloak and bonnet ready to slip on, Sophie,' he said. 'Somebody might ask for a ride. And if we have to give anyone a lift you'll have to be a lady again.'

'I'd sooner be almost anything in the world than a lady,' sighed Sophie, remembering the tickling veil. 'But I'll do it if you say so.'

Thus, driving his own farm-wagon coach, with a scarecrow and a seal for passengers, John Dolittle successfully completed the next stage in his strange journey. They passed very few people, and no one asked for a ride.

A little further on, the plough horse stopped. 'This is Redhill Farm on the right,' he said. 'Wait till I call Joe.'

Then he went close to the hedge beside the road and neighed softly. Presently there was a scampering of hoofs and his friend, a much younger horse, poked his head over the hawthorns.

'I've got John Dolittle here,' whispered the

plough horse. 'He wants to get to the Bristol Channel in a hurry. Can you take him?'

'Why, certainly,' said the other.

'You'll have to use a wagon of your own,' said the plough horse. 'I must get mine back to the barn before my farmer wakes up. Got a cart or something anywhere about the place?'

'Yes, there's a trap up in the yard. It'll be faster than a wagon. Come over this side of the hedge, Doctor, and I'll show you where it is.'

Then, hurrying before it became too light, they made the exchange. Madame Sophie was transferred from a farm wagon to a smart trap. The old plough horse, after an affectionate farewell from the Doctor, started back with his own wagon, driven by his scarecrow propped up on the front seat. At the same time, John Dolittle and Sophie were carried at a good, swift pace in the opposite direction, towards the Channel.

John Dolittle and Sophie now found that the worst part of their troublesome travelling was over. Gradually they began to see the lights of the seaport town twinkling in the distance. The land sloped upwards to the cliffs overlooking the Bristol Channel.

Not wanting to involve the Redhill horse in

what might still be a dangerous venture, the Doctor drew up the reins and lifted Sophie down from the trap.

'Thank you for your kindness,' he said to the horse. 'We had better go on foot from here. You will just have time enough to return without being missed.'

'Not at all,' replied the Redhill horse. 'It was my proud pleasure to help you, Doctor Dolittle. Goodbye!'

The Doctor made Sophie keep her bonnet on, and he had her cloak ready to throw over her at any minute because there were many roads to cross and farmhouses to pass upon the way. About a mile had to be covered before they would reach the top of the long slope and come in sight of the sea beyond the cliffs. Sophie did not complain, but the uphill going was telling on her terribly. And when at last they came to a level stretch at the top, and the wind from the Channel beat in their faces, Sophie was absolutely exhausted and unable to walk another step.

The distance now remaining to the edge of the cliffs was not more than a hundred yards. Hearing the voices of people singing in a house nearby, the Doctor began to fear that they might yet be discovered - even with the end of their long trip in sight. So with poor Sophie in a state of utter collapse, he decided there was nothing for it but to carry her the remainder of the journey.

As he put the cloak around her he saw the door of the house open and two men come out. Hurriedly he caught the seal up in his arms and staggered with her towards the edge of the cliffs.

'Oh,' cried Sophie when they had gone a few yards, 'look, the sea! How fresh and nice it sparkles in the moonlight. The sea, the sea at last!'

'Yes, this is the end of your troubles, Sophie,' the Doctor panted as he stumbled forward. 'Give my regards to the herd when you reach Alaska.'

At the edge, John Dolittle looked straight downwards to where the deep salt water swirled and eddied far below.

'Goodbye, Sophie,' he said with what breath he had left. 'Goodbye, and good luck!'

Then, with a last tremendous effort, he threw Sophie over the cliff into the Bristol Channel.

Turning and twisting in the air, the seal sped downwards - her cloak and bonnet, torn off her by the rushing air, floating more slowly behind. And as she landed in the water the Doctor saw the white foam break over her, and the noise of a splash gently reached his ears.

'Well,' he said, mopping his brow with a handkerchief, 'thank goodness for that! We did it, after all. I can tell Matthew that Sophie reached the sea.'

Then a cold shiver ran down his spine. A heavy hand had grasped his shoulder from behind . . .

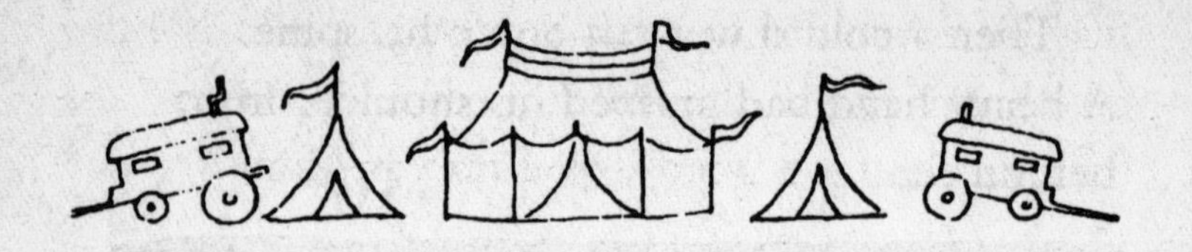

13. *Caught in the Act*

John Dolittle, turning about slowly, found a large man grasping his collar. He wore some kind of a sailor-like uniform.

'Who are you?' asked the Doctor.

'Coastguard,' said the man.

'What do you want? Let go of my coat.'

'You're arrested.'

'What for?'

'Murder.'

While the Doctor was still trying to recover from his astonishment, he saw more people coming across the downs. When they came close he saw they were two men and a woman.

'Have you got him, Tom?'

'Yes. Caught 'im right in the act.'

'What was it?'

'A woman,' said the coastguard. 'I grabbed him just as he threw her over the cliff. Jim, you run down to the station and get the boats out. You may be in time to save her yet. But I doubt it. I'll take him along to the jail. You come on down there or send me word if you find anything.'

'It'll be his wife,' said the woman, peering at the Doctor in awe and horror. 'Murdered his wife! You Bluebeard! He ought to be ashamed of 'isself,' said the woman. She gazed over the edge of the cliff with a shudder. 'I wonder if they will find 'er. Seems to me almost as though

I could see something floating on the water down there. Poor creature! Well, that's the end of her troubles. Maybe she's better off than she was, married to him, the brute!'

'It wasn't my wife,' said the Doctor sullenly.

'Who was it, then?' asked the coastguard. 'It was some woman - 'cause I seen you carrying her in your arms.'

To this the Doctor decided, after a moment of thought, to say nothing. Now that he was arrested he would probably have to admit in the end that it was Sophie he had thrown into the sea. But until he was compelled in court to tell the whole story, it seemed wiser to keep silent.

'Who was it?' the man repeated.

Still the Doctor said nothing.

'It was his wife all right,' said the woman. 'He has a wicked eye. I'll bet he has five or six wives stowed away somewhere - waiting for their doom, poor things.'

'Well, he don't have to answer,' said the coastguard. 'It's my duty to warn you,' he said very grandly, turning to the Doctor, 'that anything you say may be used in evidence against you. Now let's go down to the court-house.'

Fortunately for the Doctor it was the early

hours of the morning. And when after crossing the downs they finally made their way into the town, they found the streets deserted. The woman had not accompanied them. And the Doctor and his coastguard reached the court-house without meeting a single soul.

Just as they were about to enter the police station next door, Jim, the other coastguard man, ran up and joined his companion, with Sophie's wet cloak on his arm and her bonnet in his hand.

'We couldn't find the body, Tom,' he said, 'but these clothes was floating at the foot of the cliff. I brought these down to you 'cause I thought you might want 'em.'

'Yes, they'll be needed in evidence,' said the other man, taking the things from him. 'Better go back and carry on with the search. I'll come and join you as soon as I've got the prisoner locked up.'

Then the poor Doctor was taken into the police station; and after his name and various particulars about him were written down in a big book, he was placed in a little stone cell with some bread and water and left to his own thoughts.

Picking up the loaf that had been provided

for him, he broke it in half and ate a couple of mouthfuls. He was very hungry.

'What good bread!' he murmured. 'Quite fresh. I must ask the jailer where he gets it. The bed isn't bad either,' he added, punching the mattress. 'I think I'll take a nap. Haven't had a decent sleep in I don't know how long.'

Then he took his coat off, rolled it up for a pillow, and lay down.

And when, about ten o'clock in the morning, the superintendent of police entered with a tall white-haired gentleman, they found the prisoner snoring loudly.

'Humph!' murmured the old gentleman in a low voice. 'He doesn't look very dangerous, does he, Superintendent?'

'Ah,' said the other, shaking his head, 'it only shows you, Sir William, what a life of crime will do. Fancy being able to sleep like that after throwing his poor wife into the sea!'

'Well, leave us alone for a little while,' said the older man. 'And, by the way, you need not mention my visit here to anyone – not for the present.'

'Very good, Sir William,' said the superintendent. And he went out, locking the door behind him.

Then the white-haired old gentleman stood looking into the Doctor's peaceful face. Presently he shook the sleeper gently by the shoulder.

'Dolittle,' he said. 'Here – John, wake up!'

Slowly the Doctor opened his eyes and raised himself on his elbow.

'Where am I?' he said drowsily. 'Oh, yes, of course, in jail.'

Then he stared at the man who stood beside him. And at last a smile spread over his face.

'Heavens above! It's Sir William Peabody, my old school friend,' he said. 'Well, well, William! What on earth brings you here?'

'I might ask you the same question,' said the visitor.

'My goodness!' murmured the Doctor. 'It must be fifteen years since I've seen you.'

'They made me a Justice of the Peace about five years ago,' said the old gentleman. 'You're due to appear before me for examination in about half an hour. What I want to hear is your version of this charge that is brought against you. You are accused of murdering your wife. I happened to notice your name on the police book. What's it all about? They tell me you were seen throwing a woman into the sea.'

'It wasn't a woman,' said the Doctor.

'What was it then?'

The Doctor looked down at his boots and fidgeted like a schoolboy caught doing something wrong.

'It was a seal,' he said at last, 'a circus seal dressed up as a woman. She wanted to escape, to get back to Alaska and her own people. So I helped her. I had to disguise her as a woman so we could travel without arousing suspicion. And the circus folk were out after me. Then just as I got her here to the coast and was throwing her into the sea so she could swim back to her native waters, one of your coastguard men saw me and put me under arrest - what are you laughing about?'

Sir William Peabody, who had been trying to suppress a smile throughout the Doctor's story, was now doubled up with laughter.

'Same old Dolittle. Still mad about animals,' he gurgled when he had partly recovered. 'As soon as they said it was your wife, I knew there was something fishy about it. And there was, all right! You do smell terrible. Now tell me: how far back on this trip of yours were you and the lady you eloped with seen? Because although we can certainly get you out of the charge of wife murder, it may not be so easy to clear you on the charge of stealing a seal. Were you followed down here, do you think?'

'Oh, no. We were not bothered by the circus folk after we got away from Ashby. Then at Shottlake we got taken for highwaymen and caused a little sensation when we travelled by coach. But after that, nobody suspected anything till . . .'

'Till you threw your lady-love over the cliff,' Sir William put in. 'Did anyone see you being brought in here?'

'No,' said the Doctor. 'No one down here knows anything about it except the three coastguardsmen and a woman - the wife of one of them, I suppose. The streets were quite empty when I was brought to the jail.'

'Oh, well,' said Sir William, 'I think we can manage it. You'll have to stay here till I can get the charge withdrawn. Then get away from this part of the country as quick as you can.'

'But what about the coastguard folk?' asked the Doctor. 'Are they still hunting for the body?'

'No, they've given it up now,' said Sir William. 'They brought back your victim's cloak and bonnet. That was all they could find. We'll say you were just throwing some old clothes into the sea - which is partly true. When I explain matters to them they won't talk - and even if they do, it isn't likely their gossip will ever reach your circus people. But listen, Dolittle: do me a favour and don't bring any more animals down here to throw over our cliffs, will you? It would get hard to explain if you made a habit of it. Besides, you'll spoil the circus business. Now you stay here till I've fixed things up officially; and as soon as they let you out, get away from this district. Understand?'

'All right,' said the Doctor. 'Thank you.'

When Sir William had gone, the Doctor started walking up and down his cell for exercise. He began to wonder how things were getting on with his household in his absence. And he was still thinking about his friends when, about half an hour later, a police sergeant appeared at the door, extraordinarily polite and gracious.

'The superintendent presents his compliments, Doctor,' he said, 'and apologizes for the mistake that was made. But it was not our department's fault. It was the coastguards who made the arrest. Very stupid of them, very. The charge is now withdrawn, Sir, and you are free to go whenever you wish.'

'Thank you,' said the Doctor. 'I think I'll go now. It's a nice prison you have here - almost the best I was ever in. Tell the superintendent he needn't apologize. I've had a most refreshing sleep. This cell would make a splendid place for writing - undisturbed and airy. But unfortunately I have matters to attend to and must leave right away. Good day to you.'

'Good day, Sir,' said the sergeant. 'You'll find the exit at the end of the passage.'

And so Doctor Dolittle set off home to find his friends who were anxiously awaiting his return at the circus. And what a story he would have to tell them!